E
Mai   Maisner, Heather
         It's my turn!

It's My Turn!

Heather Maisner

ILLUSTRATED BY Kristina Stephenson

KINGFISHER
BOSTON

One morning Amy and Ben's friends came over to play. Mom and Dad put up a tent in the backyard, and then they went inside to work on the house.

Amy and her friend Lucy filled the tent with teddy bears.

"Let's have a teddy bears' tea party," said Amy, and they ran inside to get the tea set.

"Honk, honk! Honk, honk," Ben cried. "Here comes the dump truck." He pulled open the tent flaps and unloaded his cars into the tent.

"Toot, toot! Toot, toot," his friend George sang out, pushing the teddy bears aside.

"Now let's get the tractors,"
said Ben, and they raced
back to the house.

Amy and Lucy carried the tea
tray carefully through the yard.
Amy opened the tent flaps and
cried, "Ben, what have you done?"

Ben rushed out of the house with his arms full of tractors.

"Out of the way," he called. "Here come the tractors."

"But the teddy bears are having a tea party," said Amy.

"They can't. This is my garage."

"It isn't."

"It is."

"Mom!" howled Amy.

Mom came hurrying to the tent.
"Calm down," she said. "Let's
see how we can sort this out so
that you can all play in the tent."

"The teddy bears were here first," Amy said quickly.

"Then suppose the teddy bears have their tea party now," said Mom. "And the cars go in there later."

Everyone agreed, and they all helped carry the cars out of the tent.

The children asked if they could have lunch in the tent. As soon as Dad put down the pizza, Amy began piling it onto her plate.

"Amy's taking too much," Ben complained.

"I'm hungry," said Amy.

"So am I. I want more." Ben reached for the food on Amy's plate.

"There's plenty for everyone," said Dad, sharing the pizza equally between them. Then they all counted together as he placed ten strawberries in each bowl.

After lunch Amy and Ben played on the computer while George and Lucy stood by watching.

George said, "I want a turn," and tried to take Ben's controls.

"Get off," Ben cried, pushing him aside.

"But we want to play too," Lucy moaned, reaching in front of Amy.

"Go away," Amy shrieked. "We're not finished."

Mom rushed in and asked, "If everyone wants to play, what do you think you could do?" They all frowned.

"We could take turns," Amy suggested.

"Good," said Mom. "And you could time how long each person plays, so you all have fun."

Later the boys raced upstairs. As they passed Amy's bedroom, George pointed to a pretty wooden box on the bed and asked, "What's that?"

"Amy's jewelry box," said Ben. "Do you want to see it?"
Soon Ben, George, and Figaro were wearing jewelry
from head to toe.

They ran outside and pranced around the tent.
"That's mine! Give it back," Amy shouted. "Dad!
Come here!"

Dad hurried to the tent and asked the boys, "How do you think you'd feel if someone took your favorite cars?"

"Very, very angry," said Ben.

"Me, too," said George.

"Well, that's how Amy feels right now," Dad said. "So what do you think you should do?"

"Give it back, I guess," Ben mumbled, as they both took off the jewelry.

"Isn't there a game that you could all play together?" Dad asked.

"We could play duck, duck, goose," suggested Lucy.

"Or catch!" said Amy.

"No, cards," said George.

"What about hide-and-seek?" said Ben. But nobody moved.

"I know," said Lucy, "let's have a treasure hunt."

"Yes!" cried Amy. "My jewelry can be the treasure."

"And my cars can be ships, and we can be pirates," said Ben.

"And Figaro's our tiger. Yippee! Let's go!" shouted George.

Soon the garden echoed with shrieks and cries as they hunted for treasures, and the tent became a castle, then a cabin, then an underground cave.

When Mom and Dad finished
working on the house, they went
out to the yard.

"It's very quiet out here,"
said Mom. They walked
up to the tent and
pulled back the flap.

Lucy, Amy, George,
and Ben were curled up
together, falling asleep.

Amy opened one eye and
said, "Thanks for the tent.
We had a fantastic day."

The publisher thanks Eileen Hayes, parenting adviser for the U.K. child protection charity NSPCC,
for her kind assistance in the development of this book.

For Nattie and Ollie—H. M.
For Guy, Joshua, and Alexandra—K. S.

KINGFISHER
a Houghton Mifflin Company imprint
222 Berkeley Street
Boston, Massachusetts 02116
www.houghtonmifflinbooks.com

First published in 2005
2 4 6 8 10 9 7 5 3 1

LIBRARY OF CONGRESS CATALOGING-IN-PUBLICATION DATA
Maisner, Heather.
It's my turn!/Heather Maisner; illustrated by Kristina Stephenson.
p. cm.—(First-time stories)
Summary: When Amy and Ben's friends come over to play in their garden
tent, it takes awhile before everyone manages to take turns and share.
[1. Sharing—Fiction. 2. Behavior—Fiction. 3. Brothers and
sisters—Fiction. 4. Play—Fiction.] I. Title: It's my turn! II.
Stephenson, Kristina, ill. III. Title IV. Series: Maisner, Heather.
First-time stories.
PZ7.M2784It 2005   23034
[E]—dc22
2004006972

ISBN 0-7534-5740-7
ISBN 978-07534-5740-5

Printed in Singapore

1TR/0704/TWP/PICA(PICA)/150MA